New 94

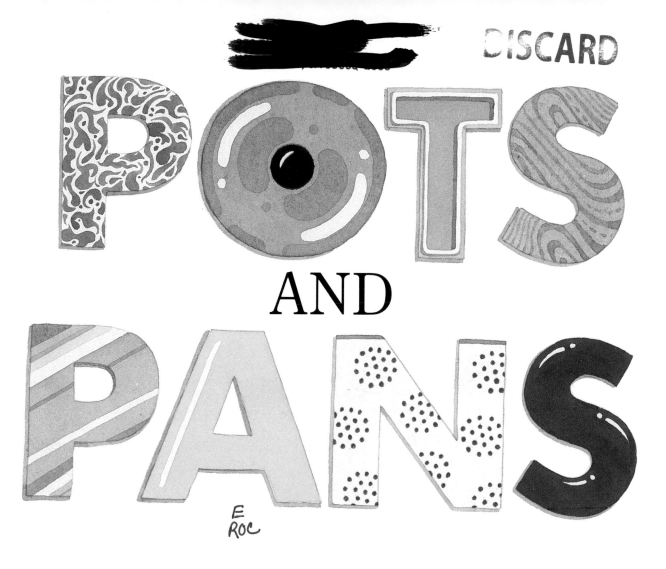

POTS AND PANS

by *Anne Rockwell*　　*illustrated by Lizzy Rockwell*

Macmillan Publishing Company　*New York* • Maxwell Macmillan Canada　*Toronto*
Maxwell Macmillan International　*New York　Oxford　Singapore　Sydney*

for Nicholas Harlow
and Juliana Joy

Macmillan Publishing Company is part of the Maxwell Communication Group of Companies.
Macmillan Publishing Company, 866 Third Avenue, New York, NY 10022.
Maxwell Macmillan Canada, Inc., 1200 Eglinton Avenue East, Suite 200, Don Mills, Ontario M3C 3N1.

First edition. Printed in the United States of America.

1   3   5   7   9   10   8   6   4   2

The text of this book is set in 30 pt. Century Oldstyle.
The illustrations are rendered in watercolor.

Library of Congress Cataloging-in-Publication Data
Rockwell, Anne F. Pots and pans / by Anne Rockwell ; illustrated by Lizzy Rockwell — 1st ed.   p.   cm.
Summary: Introduces the shiny, colorful utensils in a kitchen cupboard, including the tea kettle, omelette pan, and cake mold. ISBN 0-02-777631-X 1. Kitchen utensils—Juvenile literature. [1. Kitchen utensils.] I. Rockwell, Lizzy, ill. II. Title. TX656.R63 1993   641.5'028—dc20   91-4976

Look what's in our kitchen—

it is full of lots and lots of pots and pans

and lots of other things.

There is a great,
big, heavy casserole,

and a black cast-iron frying pan.

There is a middle-sized saucepan

and a little butter warmer.

There is a wire whisk
and a red mixing bowl,

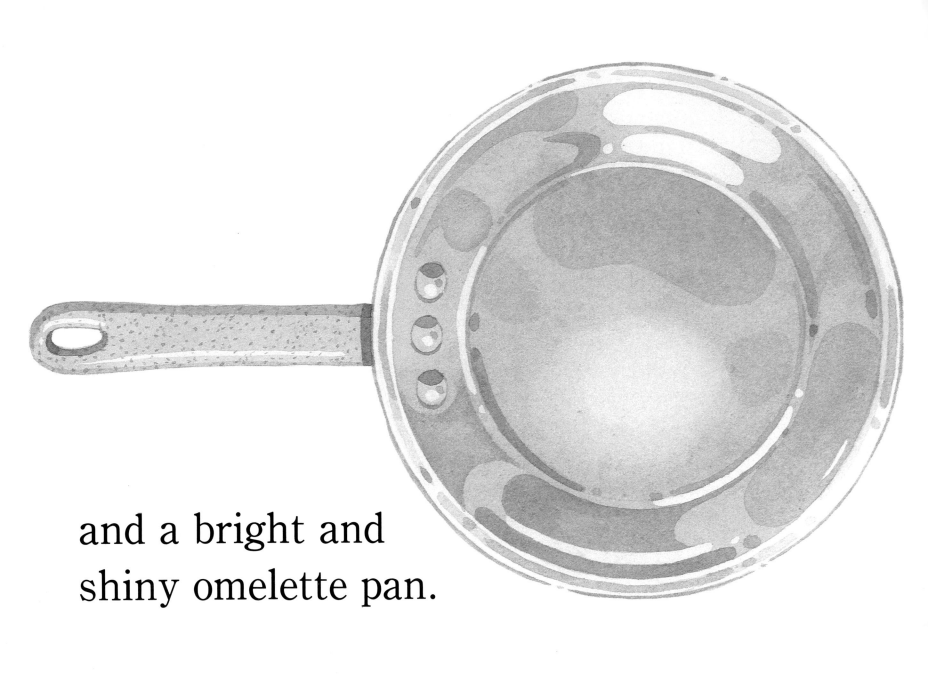

and a bright and
shiny omelette pan.

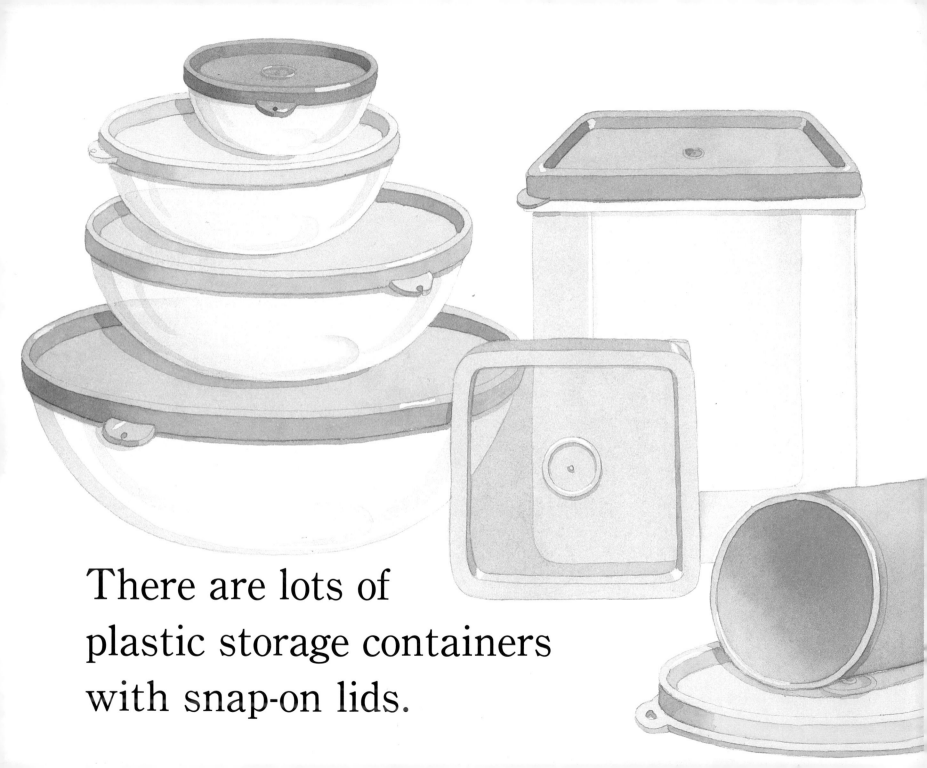

There are lots of
plastic storage containers
with snap-on lids.

Some are square and some are round.

There is a tea kettle,

and a pair of skinny chopsticks
and an enormous wok.

There are little measuring spoons
hanging on a ring
and a clear plastic measuring cup.

How many wooden spoons
are in our kitchen cupboard?

This is the cake mold
for baking fancy cakes,

and this is our wooden rolling pin.

A colander and strainer

are inside the cupboard, too.

Hooray for

pots and pans!

Will you play, too?